BY ALI BOVIS   ILLUSTRATED BY JEN TAYLOR

SYLVIE
Earth Day Extravaganza

TENTS &
TENTS

I ♥ EARTH!

Calico
An Imprint of Magic Wagon
abdobooks.com

FOR MY PANDAS- FOR ALWAYS BELIEVING IN
SYLVIE, AND IN ME. —AB

FOR MARC AND MY FAMILY —JT

abdobooks.com

Published by Magic Wagon, a division of ABDO, PO Box 398166,
Minneapolis, Minnesota 55439. Copyright © 2020 by Abdo Consulting
Group, Inc. International copyrights reserved in all countries. No part
of this book may be reproduced in any form without written permission
from the publisher. Calico™ is a trademark and logo of Magic Wagon.

Printed in the United States of America, North Mankato, Minnesota.
102019
012020

 THIS BOOK CONTAINS
RECYCLED MATERIALS

Written by Ali Bovis
Illustrated by Jen Taylor
Edited by Bridget O'Brien
Art Directed by Candice Keimig

Library of Congress Control Number: 2019942035

Publisher's Cataloging-in-Publication Data

Names: Bovis, Ali, author. | Taylor, Jen, illustrator.
Title: Earth day extravaganza / by Ali Bovis ; illustrated by Jen Taylor.
Description: Minneapolis, Minnesota : Magic Wagon, 2020. | Series: Sylvie; book 4
Summary: Sylvie's excitement for the upcoming Earth Day Extravaganza fizzles when her
    cousin, the non-recycler, visits, and she worries about not only saving the entire world, but
    the extravaganza itself.
Identifiers: ISBN 9781532136542 (lib. bdg.) | ISBN 9781644943229 (pbk.) | ISBN 9781532137143
    (ebook) | ISBN 9781532137440 (Read-to-Me ebook)
Subjects: LCSH: Earth Day--Juvenile fiction. | Cousins--Juvenile fiction. | Ecology--Juvenile
    fiction. | Recycling (Waste)--Juvenile fiction. | Teamwork in social service--Juvenile
    fiction. | Self-assurance--Juvenile fiction. | Friendship--Juvenile fiction.
Classification: DDC [Fic]--dc23

TABLE OF CONTENTS

THE POLLUTER

Sylvie's roller coaster car ticked up the tracks. The theme park spread out below:

The top of the carousel.

The inside of the spinning cups.

The mast of the pirate ship.

Best of all, Sylvie could see the wildlife conservation-themed petting zoo, rainbow-colored recycling bins, and stellar "No Plastics" posters.

Sylvie filled her lungs with popcorn-scented air. The roller coaster car slowed. The big dip was coming!

Sylvie double-checked her seat belt and tightened her hat and sunglasses. Raising her hands, she swiveled toward her seatmate, Sammy. "Ready?"

Sylvie's best friend looked up from his petting zoo pamphlet. He shoved it in his pocket, pressed down his visor, and raised both hands. "Ready!"

The car slipped over the edge and flew down the tracks. "Ahhhh!" Sylvie screamed.

What a stellar way to kick off spring break! she thought. The wind pulled her smile even wider with each twist and turn of the car.

It was going to be the best spring break. First, a day at her favorite theme park. Then a week planning the Sea View Earth Day Extravaganza—a dream vacation!

Back on the ground, Sylvie high-fived Sammy and her little brother, Henry. He was eating a caramel apple while he waited with their parents.

Sylvie fanned herself as they all walked toward the haunted mansion. "Is it always this hot so early in the spring?"

"I don't think so," Sammy said.

"It must be global warming," said Sylvie. "The hot temperatures are a danger to humans, plants, and animals."

Sammy tugged on one of his paw-print patterned socks. "Animals, too?"

"Yep," Sylvie replied. She spun the "Reduce, Reuse, Recycle" pin on her shirt. "But we can help."

Sammy straightened his glasses and nodded.

The line at the haunted mansion stretched even longer than the line at Sea View Scoops on all-you-can-eat free toppings day. "No time like the present to start planning!" She pulled out her pocket notebook and nudged Sammy and Henry.

"We've only got a week until Earth Day. A week to stop global warming and all the other problems facing the planet!"

"You mean there are more problems?" asked Henry.

They inched forward a little.

"Yep! For example, from the top of the roller coaster I spotted a mountain of trash, right outside the park gates," Sylvie said. "There's too much trash everywhere. But we can help fix that, too!"

Something grazed Sylvie's knee. An empty cookie bag was drifting to the ground. Sylvie picked it up and returned the bag to the little boy who had dropped it. He turned over in his stroller ahead of her in line.

He had littered, and he didn't care one bit! "Come on!" Sylvie waved a finger and spoke in her most serious, grown-up voice. "Don't pollute!"

The polluter must have felt bad for polluting. He kicked his legs and cried the entire rest of the line.

Sylvie whispered to Sammy and Henry. "Little kids are the future. They're the ones we're doing this for!"

"The animals too?" asked Sammy.

"And the animals too," Sylvie said.

"OK. I'm in," Sammy replied.

"Me too!" said Henry.

"Stellar!" Sylvie cheered.

Saving the planet would be a big task. It might even be their most important effort yet. After all, they had planned the best Make a Difference Day helping the Sea View Animal Shelter, organized Sea View's biggest ever winter coat drive, and led the charge to save Sea View Beach.

The haunted house butler cleared his throat. "How many riders?" he asked.

A huge laugh erupted from Sylvie's dad. "I guess we're eight now."

Silly Dad, Sylvie thought. She counted: One, Sammy. Two, Henry. Three, Mom. Four, Dad. Sylvie made five. "We're five riders. Not eight."

Sylvie's eyes popped at the sight of something unexpected between the ghost-horse carriage and the tombstones. Her knees buckled. And she screamed like she was back on the roller coaster.

HITCHHIKING GHOSTS & VAMPIRE LITTERERS

"Ahhhhh!" Sylvie screamed. What a surprise to see her favorite cousin, all the way from New York.

"Justin!" Henry yelled.

Justin smiled under the brim of his worn-out navy Yankees cap. "Three Schwartzes!" he cheered, pointing to his chest.

Of course Justin would remember to wear their special T-shirt, the one with a funny photo of him with Sylvie and Henry. "Three Schwartzes," read the caption.

"Hey, hey!" called Justin's dad, Sylvie's uncle Don, waving a cotton candy.

Justin's mom, Sylvie's aunt Bonnie, blew kisses with both hands.

Sylvie and Henry squeezed under the turnstile. Mom and Dad could hold their place in line for a minute. They raced to their cousin. "Three Schwartzes!" they shouted, hugging.

Up close, something about Justin seemed different. Same Yankees hat.

Same special T-shirt. Same checkered skateboarding sneakers.

But what was beside him? Sylvie had never seen that before. Yikes!

What was that non-biodegradable, planet-wrecking Styrofoam cooler doing there? Sylvie twirled the bottom of her "Save the Planet" top.

She pointed at the cooler. "What's that?"

"Excellent Yankees stickers, I know!" Justin replied, pulling out a water.

But it was the cooler that the stickers were stuck on that Sylvie couldn't look away from. Plus, was Justin holding a plastic bottle? A non-biodegradable plastic bottle?

Double yikes! Everyone knew non-biodegradable materials like Styrofoam and plastic were harmful to the environment.

Sylvie thought things could not get any weirder. Then Justin took a sip with a plastic straw.

Triple yikes! This was a lot to take in.

Justin twisted the bottle cap closed and turned to Sylvie. "Well, good surprise?"

Sylvie knew she should be happy. But the plastic and Styrofoam clouded her brain. She felt dizzy as if she'd just gotten off the spinning cups ride.

She focused on the Three Schwartzes T-shirt to steady herself. Justin may have been careless about how his actions could impact the environment, but he was still Justin.

Her three-years-older cousin, who had taught Sylvie how to boogie board. Ride a bike. Roast a marshmallow. Improve any meal with rainbow sprinkles.

Sylvie's head cleared enough to respond. "The best surprise!" She'd worry about the other stuff later.

Sammy walked over and joined them.

"Sammy!" said Justin, stretching his fist out for a bump.

"Kids!" Sylvie's dad called. "Let's go."

Sylvie turned to her cousin, her brother, and her best friend. "C'mon," she said. "We can ride together."

"Excellent," said Justin. He took one last sip of water.

Always good to hydrate, Sylvie thought. Especially with all this global warming.

She'd remind Justin later to carry a reusable bottle and straw. Not plastic! And to use the convenient water bottle filling stations throughout the park.

"Oh look, you can recycle there," she said, pointing.

"It's all good. Let's go." Justin tossed the bottle in the trash bin.

The trash? No! How could her favorite cousin have done something so wrong? Sylvie felt something strange. Like a stab in her side. A knife through her heart.

Before Sylvie could say anything, a

haunted buggy bumped the back of her legs. She climbed in, buckled up, and gripped the handlebar.

As the ride whisked them inside, a hitchhiking ghost danced in front of Sylvie's nose. Justin made faces and put up his fists. "You want to haunt my little cousin?" he taunted. "You'll have to go through me!"

The ghost vanished in a puff of green smoke. Sylvie laughed. Recycling crimes aside, Justin was still her favorite cousin.

The haunted buggy spun circles on

its tracking, seemingly floating over a giant ballroom. Ghosts twirled and dipped. An old-fashioned waltz blasted over the speaker.

"Did you tell Justin about the big day?" Sammy yelled over the music.

Justin shook his head and yelled, "What big day?" Then he pulled out a stick of bubble gum, balled up the wrapper, and tossed it at a vampire.

Sylvie gasped. Had Justin seriously littered into the vampire's coffin?

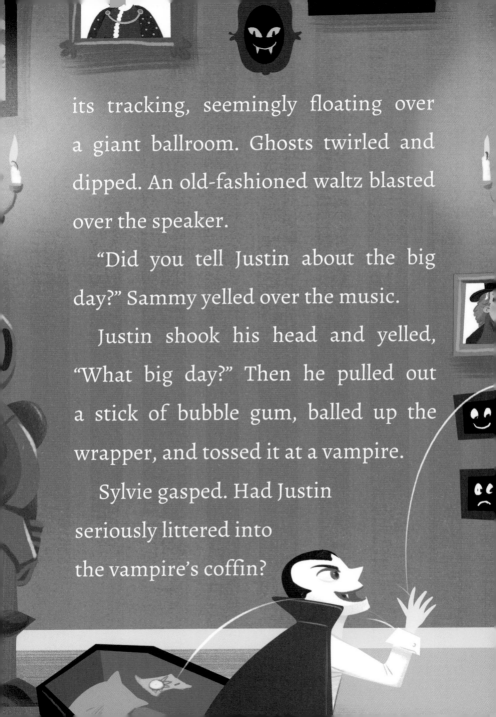

She felt as though all the blood had been sucked out of her. Justin may have been her best cousin. But could he also be the Earth's worst enemy? Like a ghost, a list of Justin's environmental crimes haunted her head.

1. STYROFOAM COOLER
2. PLASTIC WATER BOTTLE AND STRAW!
3. TRASH BIN INSTEAD OF THE RECYCLE BIN
4. LITTERING THE VAMPIRE COFFIN

Maybe she shouldn't mention her plans. "Oh, it's nothing," Sylvie said.

"Nothing?" asked Sammy. "On the pirate ride earlier, you said the future of the world and the entire galaxy depended on it."

The haunted buggy lurched to a stop.

SAVE THE EARTH

"What was Sammy talking about earlier? The future of the galaxy?" asked Justin. They had dropped Sammy off and were pulling into the Schwartzes' garage that night.

Sylvie didn't answer. It had been an awesome day at the theme park, but she wasn't sure if she should let Justin in on her Earth Day plans. What if he didn't care and messed everything up?

Sylvie, Justin, and Henry climbed out of the back seat and followed their families inside the house. Snickers, the Schwartzes' adopted puppy, galloped over to greet them.

Phew! Perfect timing, Sylvie thought. She could introduce Justin to Snickers. Then he would forget about all these questions. Sylvie leaned over and hugged the dog. "Snickers, this is Justin. Justin, Snickers."

"Woof!" Snickers held up a paw.

Justin kneeled and shook Snickers's paw. "Welcome to the family," he said.

He turned to Sylvie. "So? The future of the galaxy?"

Sylvie filled Snickers's water bowl at the kitchen sink and tried to figure out what to say. She couldn't keep her plans from him. Enemy of the Earth or not.

After all, everyone knows change starts with one person. To save the Earth, Sylvie would start with Justin.

"It's Earth Day next week," she said. She pointed to the calendar hanging above the bread basket.

Justin didn't even look up. He just kept digging around the refrigerator.

Sylvie went on. "Earth Day is like a celebration for our planet. But as you may know, our planet has lots of problems. Global warming and too much trash and pollu—"

BOOM! Thunder interrupted Sylvie's speech. "More extreme weather," she muttered. "This is a perfect example—"

SNAP! A branch whipped off a tree.

"Uh-huh," said Justin, grabbing a bag of apples. He did not seem concerned by the weather.

"There are tons of things people can do to help," Sylvie said. "Even kids."

Justin nodded, juggling the apples.

Sylvie cleared her throat and inhaled before her pitch. "I'm planning the biggest Earth Day celebration of all time. A day to save the entire planet. The Sea View Earth Day Extravaganza."

Thump! Thump! Thump! The apples hit the tile floor.

"An extravaganza?" asked Justin. "Like a party? I'm in!"

"Stellar!" Sylvie said.

But inside she thought, *how did I get through to him so quickly?* Then she remembered Justin loved the Earth's rocks for climbing, mountains for snowboarding, and ocean for surfing. He'd want to protect them.

"We can get started tomorrow," Sylvie said. "Night!"

The next morning, someone knocked at the backyard gate. Sylvie jumped off her swing and peeked through.

Neon pink puffball fluff got into her eye. She knew who this was.

Sylvie swung the gate open. Her previous lemonade stand partner's "A+ Always" bracelet sparkled in the sun.

Sylvie handed Camilla a meeting

agenda. "Everyone should be here soon. Thanks for coming."

Camilla examined the agenda. "I assume this is recycled paper?"

"Of course," Sylvie scoffed. As if she'd ever use non-recycled paper!

"Good," said Camilla. "I have a very busy day with extra credit homework. But I figured I'd help. The future of the planet is quite important to me."

It was great her former best friend shared her concerns about global warming, pollution, the destruction of the Earth's rain forests, and the threat to animals. Plus, Sylvie had to admit, Camilla had been pretty helpful lately, supporting Sylvie's efforts to save the world.

Camilla went on. "With all the extra credit I'm earning, I'll probably be honored with some best-student-ever award. I need the Earth to be around when it's time for the big ceremony."

Really? Sylvie thought. That was why the planet's future was so important?

The patio door swung open. Sylvie's dad carried a platter and placed it on the table. "Hi, girls."

Snickers sprinted over.

"Good boy," Sylvie said, scratching behind his ear. She tossed him a snickerdoodle and took one for herself, too. "Thanks, Dad."

"Sure!" Sylvie's dad replied. "Mom just answered the front door. The other kids are arriving. Have a great meeting, girls."

As Sylvie's friends filed into the backyard, Sylvie stepped inside and called for Justin. But he didn't answer. Where could he be?

"Squee!"

Screeching sounds echoed from across the house.

"Haaaaaa!"

Sylvie raced to the window, opened the shutters, and scanned the front lawn. The sounds were coming from outside.

Oh no! Sylvie inched back. *He wouldn't!*

WATER FIGHT!

PST! PST! PST! Water pounded the windowpanes. Henry shrieked as he was drenched. He grabbed the garden hose from Justin and returned fire.

Sylvie gasped. Had Justin really started a water fight? Was he really wasting that precious resource during her Earth Day meeting?

Snickers dashed outside through his dog door and chased the boys.

Sylvie banged on the glass. "Henry! Justin!" she screamed. "Snickers!"

No use.

Camilla, Josh, Nick, Tori, Lori, and the rest of her friends had walked around to the front. Everyone started grabbing for the hose and spraying each other.

Sylvie's mom came into the living room, her back to the windows. "What are you doing inside, sweetie? Aren't your guests in the backyard?"

Not even close, thought Sylvie. She pointed to the window. "They're all in the front now. Wasting water!"

Sylvie's mom turned to look and covered her mouth with her hand. Sylvie could tell she was trying not to laugh.

Sylvie pushed her palm into her forehead. So much for her mission to save the Earth. For Sylvie to save the planet she would have to save Earth Day first.

She hurried outside and turned off the spigot. "Sylvie!" Justin smiled, tilted his head, and shook water out of his ear. "You missed all the fun."

Fun? How could he think that? Then Sylvie remembered. Justin hadn't been able to fly to California for her water-conservation themed birthday party.

Maybe he really just didn't know about the importance of conserving water. And the water fight did look like fun. Sylvie took a deep breath.

Sometimes change takes time and patience. And for the Earth, Sylvie would do anything.

"It might have been fun," Sylvie said. "But we have drought problems here in California. And water is one of our planet's most precious resources. All over the world, people should never waste water."

"I hadn't thought about that," said Justin.

"Now you know," she said. "Anyway, everyone is here to meet about Earth Day. Can you dry off so we can start?"

"Sure, and I'm sorry," said Justin. He put the bucket down and rested the hose on its holder. "Come on, Henry," he added, leading Henry toward the house.

Sylvie wiped water off her clipboard. She turned on her megaphone and faced her friends.

"OK people. The meeting is in the back. Let's move!"

Sammy walked over balancing a box and a handful of cookies. "Fluffy wanted some fresh air," he said. "I hope it's OK that I brought my spider."

Sylvie waved her finger at the tarantula in the box. "Of course! It's Fluffy's planet too."

Henry propped open the screen door, dripping. "Sylvie!" he yelled. "Mr. Twist 'n' Shout is on the phone."

"Ask if he's coming to the meeting," Sylvie yelled, passing out agendas. "And tell him thanks again for donating his performance this weekend."

Henry cradled the phone. He stuffed cookies in his mouth, listening.

Sylvie lifted her shoulders and opened her palms. "Well?"

"He has an emergency 'Talk Like a Pirate Day' rehearsal," Henry yelled. "He can't make it today. But he's in for the Earth Day Extravaganza."

"Stellar!" said Sylvie. If only the meeting could get started. She turned up the megaphone's volume and shouted to her brother. "Now dry off!"

Finally, people were seated at the picnic table.

Sylvie scanned her checklist. "I trust that you've all spent five hours after school, every day, plus all day on weekends working on your projects.

Would anyone like to give the first update?"

Josh raised his hand. "The car-free day is coming along great," he said.

"Most of the grown-ups we spoke to agreed to keep their cars at home and use alternate methods of transportation to reduce air pollution," said Josh's brother, Nick. "A few said they needed them. They promised to ride together."

"Stellar!" She spun around, looking for more good news.

Tori and Lori were playing with Snickers. "How are plans for the community garden?" Sylvie asked. "Did you get volunteers signed up for the fifteen-minute shifts? We need to fill twenty-four hours!"

"Almost," said Tori, grabbing an endangered lemur stuffy from Snickers and tossing it.

Sylvie knew it would be a lot of planting. And watering. And reading to the seedlings. But the Earth needed it!

Lori rubbed Snickers's head. "Just twenty-three more hours to go."

"Stellar!" Things were really moving along now.

But then, from the corner of her eye, Sylvie noticed two figures shuffling across the patio.

She dropped her megaphone. It rolled under the table. Snickers growled and hid behind Sylvie's legs.

For a split second, Sylvie was sure two mummies from the haunted house had followed her home!

Sylvie's jaw dropped at the sight of the two mummies. Could they have escaped from the haunted house?

Nope! One of them giggled. By the looks of them, these mummies escaped from the paper towel factory. They must have been three rolls thick!

"Oooh!" said Malik.

"Spooky!" said Zaki.

Snickers growled from his hiding spot.

"It's just Henry and me," said Justin, peeling away layers of paper product.

All that paper, Sylvie thought. *All those trees. So much waste.* She sighed heavily and slid into a lounge chair, discouraged.

Justin crumpled up his paper towels and shoved them into the garbage can. "Come here, Henry. I can unwrap you."

Sylvie stared at the garbage can, speechless.

"Oh, sorry!" said Justin. He grabbed the paper towels from the trash bin. "I should recycle these, huh?"

Well, he was trying. "Actually, paper towels can't be recycled," Sylvie replied. "But they can be composted."

She was going to need more patience than she had realized to teach him. Just as he had been patient with her, when he taught her to ride a bike. "Don't you realize how wasteful that was?"

"I guess I didn't think about it," Justin replied. "We were playing around, and the paper towels were right there. We thought it would be funny. Sorry!"

She didn't know what to say to that. There was nothing funny about wasting paper. "Sorry," said Henry, making a puppy-dog face.

Sylvie nodded. They had apologized and she needed to move on.

Then a neon pink puffball ponytail band caught her eye. Ooh, the booths!

She couldn't wait to hear Camilla's update. Plus, it could take her mind off of the paper towels. But why hadn't Camilla blurted her report out?

Sylvie looked at Camilla. "How are the booths coming?"

Camilla fidgeted with her bracelet. "I made arrangements for everything: The 'build a birdhouse' booth. The 'pin the do-not-disrupt-the-wildlife sign on the endangered-animal habitat' booth. The 'write a letter to your elected official asking them to protect the planet' booth. And the 'decorate a recycle bin in your favorite color' booth. I made plans for them all!"

"What about the 'guess the number of banana peels in the food compost' booth?" Sylvie let out a breath she hadn't known she'd been holding.

Camilla nodded. "Obviously." She continued. "But the booth equipment company got the wrong date."

"Oh no! They couldn't have!" Sylvie's heart galloped.

Camilla pinched up her face. "Yeah. They got the date wrong by a week. So none of their equipment is available."

"Oh no!" Sylvie said. "Did you tell them about the Earth Day Extravaganza? How this was the one day of the whole year where we can save the planet?"

"I did." Camilla hung her head.

Sylvie could feel her cheeks turning hot. The booths were a most stellar part of the extravaganza. What would they do now?

"Is something wrong?" called Justin. "Want to break for some waves? There should be some good ones ahead of the storm this weekend."

Waves? How could Justin think about

surfing at a time like this? And another storm? What storm? Not on Earth Day! Sylvie needed time to think. "Let's take five, people," she said.

Sylvie would make a new plan. She unzipped her backpack and pulled out her ideas binder.

"Cool stickers," said Justin.

Sylvie looked at her stickers. Her eyes lingered on the one between "Pandas Forever" and "Keep Calm + Save the Earth."

"Every day is Earth Day," the sticker read.

That was it! The new stellar idea she needed!

Yes, Earth Day was an important day. But everyone needed to look after the planet every day. And that's exactly what Sylvie and her friends must do. She looked at her house and realized just where to start: at home.

Sylvie shared the plan and everyone marched off to "go green" at their homes.

The rest of the day at the Schwartzes passed in a flash of energy-efficient light bulbs and banana peels.

The next morning, in the kitchen, Sylvie left an urgent voice mail for Sammy. Then she helped her mom prepare breakfast.

Sylvie was feeding Snickers when Justin and Henry walked in. "Good morning!" Sylvie said. "There are extra sprinkles in the cabinet."

"Excellent," said Justin.

"Don't forget to add your banana peels to the compost bin," Sylvie said. She glanced at the clock on the wall. Two whole minutes had passed and no call back from Sammy yet.

"Will do." Justin poured syrup over his rainbow-sprinkled-scrambled eggs.

Sylvie paced. She worried Sammy wouldn't get her message.

On the bright side though, she felt a little relieved about Justin. It turned out he could be a great help after all. It was thanks to him that she'd noticed her "Every Day is Earth Day" sticker.

Justin took his last bite. "I'm going to shower," he said, standing up.

"Don't forget, be quick. Save water," said Sylvie.

As Justin disappeared down the hallway, three loud knocks and one soft one rattled the front door. Sammy's special knock.

"Woof!" Snickers darted to the door.

Sylvie followed and pulled Sammy inside. "Thank goodness you're here!"

"I got your message. I brought over all the paper I have," said Sammy. "What's the emergency?"

ACT NOW!

Sylvie grabbed the notepads. "Thanks! I'm all out of paper to make signs. We can make lots now."

"Signs?" asked Sammy. "Are we having a protest? I didn't know we were doing that today. I do have two protests you invited me to on my calendar. But those are next month."

"Nothing to protest today," said Sylvie. *Yet,* she thought.

Sammy scratched behind Snickers's ears. "What are the signs for?"

"For around the house," Sylvie answered. "At first, my family did a great job going green. But now they keep forgetting!"

"Oh?" asked Sammy.

Sylvie cleared the counter. "Last night, Mom left the lights on. Uncle Don forgot to unplug the coffee maker. Henry threw leftover pizza crust in the garbage. I've been telling everyone that going green begins at home. Sometimes it can be hard to remember."

"Yeah," said Sammy.

"We need to make signs." Sylvie popped off a marker cap. "Signs to remind people to go green, every day, and exactly how!"

"Great idea." Sammy flipped through the pads. "This one is my favorite. It's from the Friends of Reptiles Alliance."

"Stellar," said Sylvie, ripping off a sheet.

Sylvie wrote in her best cursive and taped the new sign next to the coffee maker. "Unplug when not in use. That means you, Uncle Don!"

Sylvie's uncle walked into the room. Her eyes followed him like an endangered Bengal tiger tracking its prey at feeding time.

"Morning," said Uncle Don. He grabbed a mug from the cabinet and walked over to the coffee maker. He read the new sign.

Sylvie reached for her kitchen megaphone. "You can also skip coffee entirely," she said. "That would save the most energy!"

Sylvie's uncle looked at her funny, grabbed a muffin, and hurried out of the room.

"It's the cursive!" Sylvie whispered to Sammy. "It works every time!"

Sammy pointed to the pantry. "Um, you might want to see this."

Sylvie peered inside. Someone had left the light on? "People!" said Sylvie. "Really?"

Sammy pulled off a sheet of paper. "Time for another sign," he said, popping the top off of a blue marker.

Sylvie grabbed some tape and hung Sammy's sign by the light switch. "Great job, Sammy. Two signs down." She looked at her notes. "Only eighty-three to go. Good thing it's recycled paper."

"Eighty-three?" Sammy asked.

Sylvie started down the hall. "Yep. And then we can figure out how many we'll need upstairs." *There are a lot of signs to be hung*, Sylvie realized. Hopefully Justin could help too.

But where was he? She checked her endangered leopard watch.

The minute hand was down by the leopard's nose. It had been a whole eight minutes since Justin had turned on the shower.

Sylvie had a bad feeling. She continued down the hall and stopped when she saw the steam seeping out the bathroom door. "No!"

How could Justin do such a thing? First all those plastics and littering. Then the water fight and paper towel wasting. Now an eight-minute shower?

Best cousin forever or not, Sylvie had almost had it with him!

Ring! Ring! Ring! The phone sounded.

"Sylvie, can you get that?" her mom called.

Eight minutes? Sylvie thought. *Who needed to shower that long? Maybe someone who had been trapped in quicksand for thirty years. But not Justin.*

"Sylvie!" her mom yelled.

"OK!" she huffed. She walked over to the receiver and brought the phone to her room. "You've reached the Schwartzes."

"Hello," a funny sounding voice said. "Did you know the planet is facing the greatest rate of extinction since we lost the dinosaurs? But you can act now."

Sylvie's eyes opened wide. "It's terrible! The animals! Plants too! Not to mention the danger to humans."

Wow. This lady really got it. Too bad Justin hadn't answered. Maybe then he would understand.

"Press one if you'd like to donate to the Endangered Animals Fund now."

"I don't know if my parents plan to donate over the phone," Sylvie said.

"But we have lots of activities planned to raise money. We're going to sell blue and green Earth colored sugar cookies, for starters."

"Press two if you'd like to hear more," the lady said.

"I don't need to hear more. I know all about it. And let me tell you, no matter what my cousin does, I'm going to be sure we make it the best Earth Day Extravaganza ever."

"Press three if you'd like to pay by credit card."

"Huh. I don't have a credit card," said

Sylvie. "Nice talking though. Thanks for calling."

"Thank you. Goodbye."

Sylvie jumped up. Forget Justin. That lady was right. Sylvie needed to "act now!" For the endangered animals and everyone else.

SPRING FLING

Sylvie ran into the hallway. "Sammy! Henry!" They hurried into her room. Henry plopped down on a beanbag. Sammy hovered over Sylvie at her desk.

"I spoke to the nicest lady. Things are bad. But we can help." Her collection of endangered animal bobbleheads bobbled, cheering Sylvie on.

Through the wall, water pulsing against the bathroom tiles drummed on. Justin must have showered at least ten minutes by now. All that water. Sylvie shook her head.

"What happened?" asked Sammy.

Sylvie pushed the power button on her computer. "If we can act to make Earth Day every day in our homes, then why not across the entire town? The country? The world!"

"True," said Sammy. Sometimes they thought so much alike, it was spooky!

Sylvie clicked open her email. "I'm going to write to the Department of Parks and Recreation. We need to add events. We need to start today. And then we can email the rest of city hall. The governor. The president!"

"Sounds great," Sammy said.

Sylvie's reusable shopping tote swayed on the bedroom knob. The door opened. Water dripped on the wooden floor. Justin stood there, dressed and drying his hair with a towel.

"Sorry it took so long. My mom showered just before me. I had to wait. What'd I miss?"

His mom was in the shower? Justin hadn't taken a ten-minute shower?

Aunt Bonnie had showered before him. Justin's shower was probably four minutes, five at the most.

The classic case of a second showerer of course! What a relief. Sylvie felt bad for doubting her cousin.

"We're acting now! Starting with a park cleanup. And then we're going to talk to local business owners and see what they can do to help save the Earth."

"Excellent," said Justin.

Sylvie heard a car door slam and peeked though her curtains. Camilla was arriving home from somewhere.

Sylvie cracked open the window. "Camilla!" she yelled. Camilla could help. "Meet at the park in an hour. And spread the word!"

Camilla gave a thumbs-up.

Huh, Sylvie thought. *Was that a little too easy?* Sylvie shrugged.

An hour later at the park, she looked at the massive crowd. So many people had showed up. Her friends, plus kids and grown-ups from across town too.

Who had called all these people? And how had they all been available on such short notice?

Sylvie noticed a sign, "Spring Fling in the Park." It was Sea View Library's annual party in the park. That's why everyone was there. And probably why Camilla had agreed to come so quickly!

Sylvie took in the view. All the books. All the shaved ice. All the potential park cleanup volunteers.

Sammy and Henry and even Camilla helped Sylvie gather everyone by the chapter books table. But not Justin.

He got in line at the shaved-ice truck. Sylvie sighed. Justin still seemed to be missing the point.

The only ice he should be worried about is the melting polar ice caps, she thought.

Sylvie shook off her disappointment. Justin would understand when he was ready. She climbed to the top of the slide and spoke through her megaphone.

"I hope everyone is having fun at this stellar Spring Fling. Once everyone has finished the library activities, I hope you join our activities too. Many of you helped clean the beach a few months ago," Sylvie started.

A flock of seagulls circled. *Squawk! Squawk! Squawk!*

Everyone looked at the famous Sea View seagulls. Sylvie pointed and winked. "Humans and birds alike." After all, the seagulls had been great partners in the town's "save the beach" effort.

Sylvie continued. "Together, we got rid of the pollution on our beach. Today, we will act by cleaning up the pollution in our parks, and all across our town, our state, and our country, too!"

"Let's do it!" said Sammy.

"Act now!" said Henry.

Sammy passed out bags for recycling paper, plastics, glass, and cans. Camilla passed out bags for trash. Lila passed out bags for dead weeds and other yard waste.

Tori and Lori passed around the community garden sign-up sheet. This way everyone could take turns and help grow fresh fruits and vegetables in the middle of their own town.

Everyone else got to work, too. Even Justin joined in after his second cup of shaved ice.

Better late than never, Sylvie thought.

Before long, the park was clean. Grown-ups gathered on blankets. They

COMMUNITY
GARDEN

82

chatted and listened to the radio. The playground was a hive of activity.

But then something faint came over the news. Sylvie leaned in to hear.

"Thanks for that report," said the announcer. "OK folks, you've heard it from W-SEA's very own Junie Spritzer. Enjoy the clear skies while you can. A storm is coming!"

EARTH
DAY
EXTRAVAGANZA

Days passed after the weather report at the park cleanup, but no storm emerged. Dark skies loomed. By Earth Day, it still hadn't rained.

On the big day, Sylvie and her friends gathered on Beach Street, under a dark morning sky. A bright colored banner announced Earth Day! Sylvie couldn't believe that after all of the planning, the event was finally here.

"OK, people." Sylvie looked at her list. "Great job making Earth Day every day. From the park cleanup, to going green at home, to the no-plastics petitions around town. We should be proud.

"Now the biggest day of all is here. The Earth Day Extravaganza begins any moment. You know your jobs. Let's do this for the Earth!"

"Woo-hoo!" cheered a clown with tricolored hair. "For the Earth!"

A smile spread across Sylvie's face. She checked "Mr. Twist 'n' Shout" off her list.

Now that her headlining act had arrived, Sylvie knew they were set. One listen to his hit "Protect the Planet and Touch Your Toes," and everyone would be fired up to do their part.

CRACK!

What was that? It sounded like the crack of a bat. Sylvie didn't remember a baseball game on the schedule.

Sammy ran over. "Was that thunder? Maybe it's the storm Junie Spritzer was talking about! Wind, rain, even hail!"

"A storm would ruin everything!" said Sylvie.

All their plans were outside. And hail. Who ever heard of hail in Southern California? "No way, not today!"

Anyway, Junie Spritzer said there was only a ninety percent chance of a storm. They had a whole ten percent chance it would stay dry.

"Shelly wouldn't come out of her shell to eat last night," said Sammy. "That usually means a storm is coming."

Uh-oh, Sylvie thought. Sammy's turtle was rarely wrong about the weather.

Sylvie looked at the slow-moving clouds. "Please, Earth, this is all for you," she whispered. "Please can you cooperate?"

She hoped for the best and made some final checks.

Signs were posted outside every shop: "No Plastics." "Recycle here." "Protect the Planet."

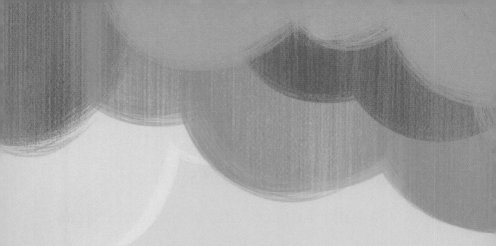

Earth-themed songs blasted over the loudspeaker. Energy-efficient light bulbs lit the streetlights.

Sylvie took in the rows of surfboards and boxes lined where the booths were supposed to have gone.

Who needed tables? Camilla had improvised. She set up surfboards balanced on cardboard boxes as flat surfaces. Posters, petitions, games, and activities were spread out on top.

"Stellar booths!" said Sylvie.

Camilla fanned out some notecards and pens. "Thanks," she said.

Sylvie turned to Tori and Lori. "Are all the community garden shifts full?"

"They are indeed," said Tori.

"Sea View Mocha Java donated coffee for the midnight to six a.m. shifts," said Lori. "The leftover coffee grounds can be used for compost."

"Great," said Sylvie. Maybe she'd let Uncle Don make coffee after all.

Sylvie walked over to Sammy and Zaki, who were setting up their area.

"Are concessions ready?" she asked.

"The Earth-colored sugar cookies and organic lemonade are ready to go," Zaki replied.

"And I will be sure no seagulls or critters of any kind get to them before our customers do," said Sammy.

Sylvie started to lead her team on some warm-up stretches. Her neighbor, Mr. Wolf, walked up. "Hi, kids! Those cookies smell delicious," he said. "Are you open for business?"

Sylvie shooed everyone into their positions. "We sure are!"

"Happy Earth Day!" said Zaki. "All sales are donated to organizations that help the Earth."

"That sounds terrific. I'll take two of each," said Mr. Wolf.

Sammy poured lemonade in Mr. Wolf's reusable Thermos. Then he wrapped his cookies in recycled paper.

Malik handed him a "10 Steps to Go Green" flyer. "Thanks for your business. And feel free to plant your flyer after you and Mrs. Wolf have read it."

"Plant it?" he asked.

Sylvie stepped in. "That's right. Our flyers are made of plantable recycled seed paper. Take a read and plant the seeds. Watch the flyer grow."

"Watch the flyer grow?" he asked.

"You got it," Sammy replied. Mr. Wolf gave a thumbs-up, took a bite of cookie, and walked away.

The rest of Sea View's citizens flowed in. Sylvie's teacher, Ms. Martin, and her husband, Mr. Martin, arrived by tandem bike. Sylvie's principal, Ms. Close, jogged over.

The Langholm Drive neighbors created a walking-bus, with everyone strolling together as a group.

Sylvie's family had gotten in the spirit, too. Her parents rolled over on rollerblades, Henry skateboarded, and Uncle Don and Aunt Bonnie rode on Sylvie and Henry's scooters.

Soon, Beach Street was packed. Everyone had showed up.

Well, almost everyone.

FLYING SUGAR COOKIES

"Where's Justin?" Sylvie asked.

Justin had been up late the night before playing her dad's drums. But where was he now? He'd made so much progress. He'd participated at the park cleanup and had been enthusiastic at the end at least! She scanned the crowd. C'mon, Justin! It's the big day!

WHOOSH! A stack of flyers blew against her clipboard.

Sylvie looked down. A drop of rain dotted its corner.

Uncle Don fastened a Band-Aid to his bloody elbow. His scooter skills must have been rusty. "Justin wanted to surf before the waves got too rough."

"He'll be by after," added Aunt Bonnie.

After? thought Sylvie. Well, she had her answer. Her favorite cousin cared more about surfing and playing drums then he did about saving the planet.

WHOOSH! A gust blew one side of the banner into the air. Wind snapped her "I heart Earth" shirt against her back.

Leaves rustled. Flags whipped in the air. Earth-colored sugar cookies flew off the table.

Justin ran over. He picked up sugar cookies scattered around the pavement and handed them to Sylvie.

"Sorry I'm late. And sorry I've been so lazy about helping. I was surfing when the wake from a ship sent all this floating garbage on me. I had to stop! I realize what you're talking about. I had no idea, Sylvie. About the pollution. About any of it! This isn't just a party. We need to protect our planet."

Sylvie's heart gave a happy thump. *Finally!* she thought.

On the main stage, Mr. Twist 'n' Shout turned on the speakers and started a sound check.

The wind howled. Justin kept talking, but Sylvie couldn't hear him. He looked serious. More serious than when the Yankees traded his favorite pitcher.

Sylvie cupped her hands to her mouth. "What?"

"I'll pick up all the litter on Beach Street. I'll plant trees on every block and post recycle bins on every corner."

He pulled a plastic soda wrapper off his shoe. "Just tell me how to help."

"Stellar!" There was her favorite cousin! It might have taken him a while, but she hadn't given up on him.

Sylvie knew just the task. She handed him a Beach Cleanup binder. Justin set his surfboard against the Tents & Tents building and hugged the binder.

BOOM! Sammy raced over. "Sylvie!"

Sylvie felt a drop of water hit her forehead. "Sammy!"

They needed to move everything indoors. Her team scrambled to clean

100

up the booths. But where in town would be big enough to move the entire extravaganza?

If only the Earth would give her a sign. Sylvie looked at the sky. "Earth! Help! Help us help you!"

10
DOUBLE RAINBOW

The sky opened. People raced in every direction to find shelter. As the rain poured, it mixed with Sylvie's tears.

Squaw! a seagull called.

Sylvie looked up and got just the sign she needed. A twenty-foot flashing sign, with three tall trees and a Tents & Tents store logo.

She waved to the seagull. "Thanks, friend!"

Tents & Tents would be perfect. It was the biggest store in all of Sea View. Everyone could fit. The activities too.

And the owner, Ms. Lauren, signed up first when Sylvie established the Sea View Task Force for Endangered Animals. Sylvie knew she would help.

Sylvie pulled her windbreaker over her head. Of all the days to leave her waterproof megaphone at home. She cupped her hand around her mouth.

"People!" she yelled. From storefront doors and umbrellas along the street, people craned their necks to see her.

"Don't leave! I've got an idea!" Sylvie shouted, pointing to Tents & Tents. She ducked inside and spoke with Ms. Lauren.

Sylvie emerged outside a minute later under an umbrella. "C'mon inside!" People hurried into the store.

Before long, the lightning and thunder had passed. But a steady rain clinked against the tin roof.

Everyone dried off in the beach towels section. Sylvie huddled with her team, Ms. Lauren, and the Tents & Tents staff.

Sammy helped Sylvie climb on a ski slope display. "Ready?" he asked, passing Sylvie her indoor megaphone.

"Ready!" Sylvie looked at the ocean of people across the store. "Let the Earth Day Extravaganza continue!"

Tori and Lori handed out umbrellas and rain boots for people to borrow while heading out to read to the seeds.

Josh and Nick helped Camilla set up new surfboard booths throughout the store.

Ms. Martin helped Zaki, Malik, and other students organize groups. People signed up to help at the sugar cookie sale table, and to clean debris off the beach, parks, and street.

The temperature had dropped to a cool sixty degrees. Sylvie distributed mini pocket warmers to everyone headed outside. Then she worked with Ms. Lauren to organize donations, rentals, and sales for alternate methods of transportation.

"Amazing job," said Sylvie's mom, checking the price tag on a bicycle.

"We're so proud of you," said Sylvie's dad, trying on a pair of sneakers.

"Show me anything but a scooter," said Uncle Don. "And can I get two more packages of bandages?"

Just then, a familiar tune blasted over the speakers. "Save the Earth and Touch Your Toes," Mr. Twist 'n' Shout belted from atop the rock wall. His performance had begun.

Bam! Bam! Bam!

A drummer in a hat played from down below. But he wasn't wearing his usual arrow-through-the-head hat. He wore a baseball hat. A worn-out navy baseball hat.

Sylvie raced through the hiking department to the rock wall.

Bam! Bam! Bam!

"Justin?"

Sylvie's cousin smiled. "Hey!"

"Three Schwartzes!" her brother screamed, hanging mid rock wall. *Ding!* went his triangle instrument.

After the performance, Henry and Justin raced over to Sylvie. Henry

grabbed some trail-mix samples set out in the camping food display.

Sylvie pointed to the drum set. "What were you doing up there?" she asked.

"Mr. Twist 'n' Shout's drummer got held up. Part of the highway is closed due to mudslides. He had to take the back roads," said Justin. "He's on the way. I figured we needed to act now. So I filled in for the first set."

Sylvie sparkled.

Hours later, the rain tapered off and the sun began to set over the ocean. The Earth Day Extravaganza was over. But acting now, to "make every day Earth Day" was here to stay!

Sylvie, Justin, Sammy, Camilla, and Henry were the last to leave the store.

"Look!" said Henry.

"What now?" asked Camilla.

"A double rainbow!" said Sammy.

"Excellent!" said Justin.

"Stellar!" said Sylvie. She'd never seen a double rainbow.

"Thanks, Earth," she whispered. "We love you, too." Then she picked up her megaphone and stretched it to the sky. "We'll see ya tomorrow!"

EARTH DAY is an annual event on April 22nd to promote clean air, land, and water. Events are held worldwide to support environmental protection. People march, pledge to protect the planet, sign petitions, and more. There are many activities kids can do on Earth Day, and every day.

For additional information, please **visit:** https://www.epa.gov/earthday